I0716683

IN MEMORY OF JAMES WRIGHT, WHOSE POEM I ATE

In Memory of James Wright,

Whose Poem I Ate

Tyler
Cain
Lacy

Chicago, IL

In Memory of James Wright, Whose Poem I Ate

Published by Long Day Press
Chicago, Il 60647
LongDayPress.com
@LongDayPress

ISBN 978-1-950987-49-8 (Paperback Edition)
ISBN 979-8-3303-1146-0 (eBook Edition)

Library of Congress Control Number: 2024937966

Layout by Joshua Bohnsack

Cover image from Russell Lee's "High school horse and his owner-trainer at the rodeo of the San Angelo Fat Stock Show, San Angelo, Texas," 1940.

Interior from Russell Lee's "Blind and thin horse on Glen Cook's farm near Smithland, Iowa," 1936.

Printed in the United States of America.
First Edition

1

"In Memory of the Horse David, Who Ate One of My Poems" takes up one page of what some readers argue consists of zero lines, lines nothing like the poem that James Wright wanted to show someone, anyone, before it disappeared into my foregut, where it was broken down (in other words, analyzed) before moving to the hindgut, before — well, I don't need to tell you how most poems end up. About that poem there isn't much worth noting, but about this poem, mistakenly seen as a blank page or a bad joke or both, there remains much to be said. Since the news just reached me that Wright has died, I thought it best to memorialize him by offering my own thoughts on his poem that came from a poem of his that I ate.

Poems are neither set-ups for punchlines, nor are they riddles. Wright knew this well before he showed up at the farm and came begging me for training. He was in search of the assurance of poetry as a possibility, and I was kind enough to appease him. I taught him to see the pasture in all of its possibility, the variety and depth of which would allow him to then shape his experiences into better poems. It was this possibility and the difference between punchlines, riddles, and poems that Wright tried to get at when, introducing this poem of his in memory of me, he announced to a crowd of dolts on February 21, 1973, "This looked as if it were a joke in my book, but it's not a joke to me." I wasn't there, obviously, but in the recording shared with me, I hear impatience in his voice that he even has to offer this prelude to the poem. "I wanted to tell you about David... I loved that horse, and —" he stutters on "and," as he always did when he was drunk, which was most of the time, "I think he loved me, too." He goes on to provide context for the poem's creation: I, the horse David, "belonged" to the poet Robert Bly and his wife Carol, whose western Minnesota farm Wright was visiting when he wrote a poem that he wanted to show them. He walked from the chicken house, where, presumably, he'd written the thing, to the farmhouse in search of his hosts, and then, still looking for anybody home, went around the back of the house, and, according to him in the recording, "of course David was wandering around. Wonderful old David. He ate the poem." There's a smile in Wright's voice as he says this last sentence. It pricks up my ears. I love the joy present in how he speaks that sentence — "He ate the poem" — rounding the vowels so softly in "poem," and the smile that's affecting his pronunciation of the word is not a cue for the crowd to giggle but a smile from understanding the wisdom — but perhaps wisdom is too heavy a word — that this fleeting moment in his life was trying to extend to him. Nonetheless, the audience mistakes his smile as the visual marker for a punchline. Laughter bounces around the crowd in what they call the Modern Languages Auditorium at the University of Arizona, whatever that combination of words is supposed to signal. "I know it sounds as if it were a joke," his voice rises above the guffaws, "but it's not a joke. No, no." As the giggles deflate, he reads the title, "In Memory of the Horse David, Who Ate One of My Poems," he says, "and here it is." But before the poem gets into the room, the audience is already laughing at what they perceive to be a joke about a paper-craving horse, a lackadaisical poet on a farm, and nothing more. Wright is silent under the laughter, the poem ends just as it gets started, and you do not hear him laughing because it is not a joke, as he has already reminded the crowd twice before they uncan their laughter anyway.

Since the poem isn't clear in the recording, I'll include it here in full before I go any further:

IN MEMORY OF THE HORSE DAVID, WHO ATE ONE OF MY POEMS

2

One of the many ironies present in this memorial of Wright is that my setting the record straight in these pages will inevitably have the undesired effect of writing over and on top of Wright's poem in memory of me. But that is the problem of the poet's, not mine, since I have no lofty goals in the business of putting words on paper for posterity. Back to the poem's context:

I am a swayback palomino who arrived at the Bly farm over twenty years ago, in August of 1959, then four years old and battered from my previous owners in what you call South Dakota and I call the pasture of bruises. That Wright (and Bly, for that matter) saw me as already "old" should raise questions not only about their adeptness as horsemen, but indeed their status as poets of so-called nature. My appearing advanced in age on the occasion that led to this poem is in keeping with what you might expect from a horse with this name, and works to elevate this poem to a sort of myth, because a horse with a name like that, a horse named David, of all names, is born to eat the work out of a poet's hand, you are likely to think. I remember Wright, baffled as he was by the name when we first met, telling me that David is a name that suggests wisdom, conviction, strength, a name that suggests the being it's attached to has a fondness for poems. That is why Wright fell so head over — no, I won't say "hooves"— heels at the prospect of what he could get out of me, not because I was a steady ambling companion with a keen sense of how to sniff out the sweetest clover in a field, yet generous in sharing my finds, but because I was given a name that has absolutely nothing to do with who I, "the horse David," was, let alone any connection to my kind, a name he thought meant something special. If you need further proof that Bly (and, by extension, Wright) were not the sharpest thorns in the field, I'm not sure you'll gain much by reading on. It was clear to me that I, David, as Wright saw me, though he wouldn't admit this to anyone, was what you would call his muse, even though he never credited me, his source for the best of his poems and ideas, in his acclaim.

3

We may not be lumped into what you call ruminants, but that holds little meaning when it comes to how we process the world. Your distinctions — monogastric or ruminant, poem or forage, for starters — appear to serve no purpose other than to perpetuate the bewilderment you have created in hopes that you will feel less lost in it. I'm sure you've heard that stupid questions lead to stupid answers. I mean, *how else* is a horse supposed to partake in poetry if not by eating it? (Even more, what does our preferred method of receiving the written word say about the futility of the lowly and passive method preferred by you, that which you call, with arrogant certitude, *reading*?) Chewing is how we process the world. Our eyes are reserved for maintaining our safety at all times.

What I am trying to get at is that even though the poem's title incorrectly identifies me as dead, which I am certainly not, a horse named David surely seems clever enough to know that he has no business consuming poems, which should make you wonder, precisely because of his wits, why a horse named David would choose to eat the poem instead of the grass sprung up around the barn where a horse is more likely to roam. (I didn't mind the aftertaste of the dog Simon's piss in the weeds and tufts, but after making the mistake of browsing there one evening after Wright and Bly had been drinking hard all day long, I vowed never to eat around the perimeter of the barn again, whether or not a wet streak was visible on the boards or a sour stench lingered over the sprouts.) The simplest way I can put it for you is that the smart animal chooses whatever provides the greatest value with the least amount of labor involved. You might assume that Wright reached out his hand without thinking, with the poem in it, toward me as a greeting, so it's no wonder, what I, a relatively affable horse in my youth, took the poem for. The problem with this assumption is that, since I was the one who ate the poem in question, I can assure you that it was terrible and offered very little, if any, nutrients. But that poem is not the subject of my rumination.

I met Wright when I first arrived, as noted above, at the farm he had made the three-hour trip from Minneapolis to return to, having already visited on numerous occasions to talk classical Chinese poems, translate Georg Trakl, and bicker over the future of American poetry with Bly. Wright had first arrived at this farm that would become his refuge for many years to come a year before me, in August of 1958. Like me, this man was also sunken low, but he was swayed from drinking his marriage and family life, as well as his job prospects in the icy academia of Minnesota, to the dregs, not sway-backed from congenital disease doubled-down with an early life of ill-fitting saddles and riders. After the publication and general success of his first collection, *The Green Wall* (1957), and already well into the final revisions, when I met him, for what would become his second, *Saint Judas* (1959), the poet felt he had said everything he was able to say from within the formal constraints of those poems. Since he didn't come to the farm seeking help with the poems that filled out those books, I can only speak to the selections from them that he shared with me during our training sessions. I remember a few disparaging comments he made about the two collections. He felt so far removed from them, he said during one of our training sessions, that he characterized the former as having been "written by a dead man," whereas the latter, he said under a drunken slur on the day it had finally gone to the printer, "seemed to leave out so much of life." Before he came stumbling to the farm, he had been searching for a conspirator in his conviction that "all poetry is formal" (my observation to Bly, which he then branded as his own, naturally, and which he passed on to Wright, who, as appears to be a pattern with all of you, had a faint notion this was the case but, without having words for it until mine came along, threw my phrase around in conversation as his own idea) and that there exists no "opposition between traditional iambic verse and free verse." Tradition wasn't the problem. His expertise in the gimmicks of rhyme, meter, and anachronistic speech had led him to a dead-end where his written work left him cold, yet he confessed to me, as he already had to Bly, that he didn't know how — or perhaps he simply didn't have the confidence required — to write beyond the constraints of what he'd mastered in his first two collections.

During this creative crisis and on the very day when the poet was writing what he deemed his last poem before giving up on poetry for good, a poem he titled — what else? — "Farewell to Poetry" (which would not be his final poem, and would instead be revised and published, in the landmark collection *The Branch Will Not Break* as "Goodbye to the Poetry of Calcium," a poem, like the others in the book, with my training all over it), a copy of a literary magazine called *The Fifties* appeared in his campus mailbox at the University of Minnesota. He knew nothing of the magazine or its editors, one of whom, Bly himself, had the printer set in bold on the inside cover, "Most of the poetry published in America today is too old-fashioned." In the foreword to this first issue of the magazine, Bly bemoans American poetry's slip back into the "old tradition" of iambic verse, which forsook, in his eyes, the hard-won gains of the Modernists of the prior decades, particularly in the elevation of everyday American speech as the language of literature. He notes that beyond the wooden American verse of the moment, contemporary models in Europe and South America writing revealed the "magnificence of suggestion and association" possible in poetry. (He had droned on and on about all of this in the barn with me, brushing my mane and cleaning out my hooves, and I finally made it clear to him, with a kick that barely missed his right knee, that I was sick of hearing it and that he should find another outlet for these ideas he got mostly from me and the others on the farm, anyway — and thus, the foreword for his new magazine.) This all seems lightning-strikingly epiphanic, of course, and Wright himself was left "wondering at the weirdness of it all," as he wrote in a rangy, arguably deranged letter to Bly that amounted to sixteen single-spaced pages detailing his sense of failure, his bewilderment about how to leave the cul-de-sac of his quaint academic poems, and his praise for what the new magazine was already doing for American poetry and for him, especially. Bly, exasperated by the letter, left it under the box elder trees where he'd been reading it, and I tucked away a few pages before he came back out and got onto me. Exasperating indeed, also languished, so depressing in tone that even the writing on the page suffered an awful slouch that was bitter to the taste and hard to digest. Bly responded to the heap, Wright told me later, with a one-sentence letter in reply: "Come on out to the farm."

By 1971, when Wright's poem in memory of me first appeared with the publication of his *Collected Poems*, there had been quite a history between not only the two poets, but also between the poet and me, although no one appears to have mentioned how, precisely, the incident between the horse and his poem occurred, when Wright set the poem commemorating this incident onto paper in the form of "In Memory of the Horse David, Who Ate One of My Poems," and when I, the horse David, allegedly passed away. No surprises there, since the focus tends mostly toward Wright's poems before this one came along (and most of those poems, with a few exceptions, such as this one, are stilted and trite attempts at poetry, if I'm honest, but that's the view of the overlooked, albeit better informed, consumer of his poems). Since Wright returned to the farm as his retreat countless times between 1958 and well into the mid-sixties (Wright claimed to others, I seem to recall hearing, that he would show up at the farm "every Friday," but that seems excessive, considering the trip involved, even for a drunk of a poet prone to exorbitance), no one bothered with the facts surrounding the occasion of the poem, so I thought it was time for me to set the record straight.

I go hello through the farmhouse. Okay. Nobody there. I am trying to find someone to show my poem to — Robert, or Carol, or the kids, anyone I come across. It is a poem I am proud of, or stuck on, or maybe no more than a poem to break the silence, to get me out of this depressive alcoholic stupor, something I can hand to somebody to say I am still here and here is what I have to show for it. This part I didn't say to the crowd in Arizona or anywhere else.

I walk to the barn and nobody there. But behind the barn stands who else. I walk up to say hello. I offer a hand to pet your neck, but you want what is in my other hand instead. Your square teeth pluck the poem from my hand and work the page into cud as I watch the veins pulse across your long jaws like the lightning in yesterday's storm. The dark bulbs of your eyes tell me that you know what you're doing, looking beyond me and the fence and the ten miles of corn fields that give way to the prairie whence you came, swaybacked already as a foal and cast off as a worthless workhorse into innumerable hands before being given up on and passed, your back swayed beyond the point of correction, to these farmers that are less farmers than poets; the kind of farmers that would christen their horse David, their Airedale the size of a greyhound Simon, and their old farmhouse with no indoor plumbing the "Odin House" after the Norse god of everything from poetry to gallows and runes to war; the kind of farmers that invite manic depressive, alcoholic poets out for a respite from a wrecked life in their chicken house turned writing shed, complete with a battered roll top desk, a kerosene stove, a stiff cot, and the baked-in smell of chicken shit that straightens depressive slouching and banishes mind-splitting hangovers and migraines.

The poem is gone before anyone can see it. Written sober for once, or maybe that is only how it was written in my recollection long after it has been lost to your chomping. The fact that it is gone is how I know, on the days when a short-lived sobriety shovels me out, that it must have been a good poem, surely one of my best. On days that same fleeting but unmanageable sobriety buries me, it is how I know the poem must have been awful.

4

I have spent the past eight years chewing on this poem in memory of me and the poem I ate. I have it memorized and have been known to recite it in my sleep. I have savored it for so long, yet it continues to sustain me. As much as the poem has become part of me, I feel that I have inhabited it, which makes sense considering I was, in a way, part of its composition. At times, I am so moved by the poem that I forget that it is me, so-called David, who is present in it. When I chew on the poem I often see not the poet and myself, but the poet and another horse named David, a horse named David who is nothing like me, frolicking through tan Midwest pastures going to seed under a bronze sun, a bronze that rhymes with the gold coat of this David's careening frame as he gallops through the western Minnesota afternoon, a golden frame that, positioned just so at the dwindling hours of daylight, cradles the setting sun in the crook of his sunken back that is nowhere near as pronounced as that of the real David, that is, me. It is a gold of sun and mane that rhymes with the poet's tar-streaked yellow teeth and nicotine-stained fingertips that flicker compliments, commands, lines of poems, and hay at the horse. I see this David having grown so close to Wright that, to the saggy-backed nag in the blissful but waning years of his life, this man was not James Wright the famous poet but just Jim, which was who he was for all of us on the farm, how I referred to him during our training sessions.

Everyone should have a reliable and voluble friend named Jim. A Jim built like a football player but as soft-hearted as a teddy bear, a balding, chain-smoking stuffed animal who can't stop spewing lines of everyone from Whitman to Po Chü-i, or the prose — whole pages regurgitated from memory — of Dickens's sentimental novels and Hobbes's baroque *Leviathan* when he drinks, which is all the time. Jim. A broken-down, tragic drunk of a poet whose life goal is to be happy, a goal attainable, for him, only through the intercession of words. But a Jim who, aside from all of these human concerns, a man that knows himself to be an animal, and so one who communes with animals and offers them poetry as sustenance — this Jim is even better. From here on out, I will refer to him as simply that, simply Jim.

But let's get out of the pasture and back to the poem.

5

Beginning from where else, the title of the poem is split, at least in the edition I ambled across when it was released eight years ago (*Collected Poems*, 1972), into two lines, "IN MEMORY OF THE HORSE DAVID, / WHO ATE ONE OF MY POEMS," which seems like a typesetter's error, or the work of a frivolous typesetter bent on turning the poem into a mere joke by emphasizing what could be taken as a sort of gag in the title's second line. Since titles of other poems throughout the collection that may be considered the same length or longer (in terms of space-taking on the page and/or words) are not enjambed but carried over into the following line with an indentation, as a line of a poem would be when it stretches beyond the margin of the physical page, the scrutinizing reader is left to call into question the book's typesetter, who, through such a small act, has changed the nature of the poem entirely and reduced it to a cocktail party joke, something Jim despised, as can be heard from that reading in 1973. I will return to say more about the title after working through the text proper of the poem.

The conspicuous consumer of this poem picks up on a theme that first appears in the title and carries through to the end: emptiness. It is clear that the poem is addressing — though not necessarily "about," since no one, not even poets themselves, as I would remind Jim, can say what poems are about other than words — two interconnected losses: that of the passing of "the horse David," as well as the disappearance of the poem that the horse ate. In the body of the poem, you are presented with a form that reflects its content (to return, briefly, to what I taught Jim about the possibility in poetry): the theme or preoccupation with emptiness is achieved through the sparse use of language to describe and address it. As you make your way through the poem, you see that its language is so calculated, its imagery evoking emptiness so precise, that you alternate, with each passing line, between considering the poem a eulogy to the horse or an elegy for a lost poem, and by the end you feel, at the end of your long jaw and in the back of your throat, where your chewing rubs its way into your thinking before your tongue slurps your forage down your long neck to the barrel of your ribs and to your stomach, that it is both and neither.

I do not mean that the poem leads to confusion, but to possibility. This is the heightened level of its imagery and metaphors, the pure music that comes off the page. The poem gives the reader permission to read it either way — as eulogy to the horse or elegy to the poem now gone — and it rewards both, but it is also neither, because the emptiness conjured by those two forms — eulogy and elegy — doesn't close off the poem. Instead, that emptiness gives way, as strange as it may sound, to happiness. This might be the defining quality of a great poem: it opens up into thought, into conversation, even contradiction, rather than closing in on itself in the face of easily attained interpretations or answers to questions that the poem cannot deal with beyond yes-or-no or illusory facts, all of which reduce a poem to little more than words on a page addressing nothing to no one. Here, however, the reader accumulates meaning as you allow the lines to build on one another until, at a certain point, you look up from the page and realize that you have been out of the world, drawn into the emptiness threaded throughout the poem's lines. At this point, you feel, deep in the marrow of the words of the poem, that you, too, knew "the horse David" intimately, that you, too, have the poem he ate memorized and are ready to dictate it to Jim, who is at a loss without it. I know some readers who experience this — what I like to call *ecstatic transfer* — after the tenth line of the poem, and others who are carried through line seventeen, and yet others who are resistant to the poem up until line twenty-six (my numbers might be slightly off, as mathematics is not exactly a horse's strength, as you can imagine — why bother counting individual strands of hay when what matters is eating the whole bale? — but you get the idea).

This brings me back to what defines a great poem: another way of thinking about this quality (admittedly rare in most poetry, especially American, before World War I, but, at least in my experience, relatively common in poetry since) is that a great poem has no predetermined ending. It invites the reader into an experience that leads to ecstatic transfer while remaining cognizant that all readers bring their own sensibilities, time, and experience (lived and literary, although perhaps those boil down to the same) to the poem, and the moment of this transfer, which tradition has taught us, erroneously, to call the end of the poem, may happen after the last line or after the first word. A great poem is the one that has its present reader's considerations and eccentricities sewn throughout its lines. In this poem of Jim's, I come to the "end" at what I calculate as the eleventh line, at which point, buried in emptiness, I read no further. This isn't to say I am defeated by the poem, or feel that the poem does me harm and therefore I decide to quit it, but that after reading the eleventh line I get jolted — I experience ecstatic transfer, which means my engagement with the poem is at its peak, and so there the poem, for me, "ends." Others I have shared the poem with experience a range of endings, and while I may disagree with some of them, sometimes vehemently — especially the ending for one reader, who insisted, slamming a hoof against a salt block until it shattered into smithereens, then throwing the book at the wall of the barn, that the poem ends before it begins, right after its title — I am not able, as a reader, to call into question the site of their ecstatic transfer, but I can attempt to sway or influence them toward the site of mine.

Okay. I was in the chicken house, and I went over to the farmhouse, and I couldn't find anybody to show my poem to. What I didn't mention was that I was too drunk to show anyone anything but myself. They weren't walking among the row of box elder trees that stood guard over the farm's north side. They weren't picking apples from the trees in front of the house, or shirking from the sun under the ash trees alongside, sunken by the brutal humidity of a Minnesota afternoon building up to an August thundershower. They weren't in the large garden, bent under indeterminate tomato vines run amok, nor were they hidden in the jurassic zucchini leaves that crawled up and conquered the trellis. The laundry on the clothes line wasn't anyone. All that was there was me, the poem that my hand, gripping proudly, was sweating the fresh ink off of, the horse I loved, and the dog Simon. It was the tranquility of you two, equine and canine, whom I'd often seen motionless, sage and so sure of yourselves like the blazing sun in the long afternoons, staring out beyond the property at the corn fields, thoughts and vision lost in the maize, or counting the maize, it all amounts to nothing is the wisdom, the lesson, what I would learn not from writing the poem my clammy hand had begun to dissolve, but from witnessing your tongue bloom from your lips to lick the poem right out of my palm. I sat in the grass next to the dog, with you standing alongside, and looked out at the cornfields of nothing. A gopher rose from the earth in front of us and Simon didn't pounce, you didn't rear up and kick, and I didn't nudge even a thought in the direction of that gopher right there.

6

"There we were, all four of us together. All I was thinking was, I can be happy sometimes...I wish I knew how to tell you," I remember Jim said of the fleeting moment between me, the Airedale Simon, the gopher, and him.

He could not quite figure out how to tell me, but I don't need the words. In fact, I don't want them. There is a certain tranquility in this reading of the poem because in this light it is ultimately a nature poem — that genre which may perhaps be best defined as poems in which people are humbled, by which I mean brought down, by the natural world. I, too, have been known to be brought low by a bold gopher. I cannot say, however, that I am a connoisseur of nature poems, since they are probably my least favorite flavor, aside from political poems, which goes without saying.

Wright considered himself a nature poet:

"It comforts me more and more to realize and to observe and to feel the great self-restoring power that the creatures in nature have while we human beings are making such a mess of things. I hope that poetry, and the poetry of nature, has a similar power." I don't know what he means by "poetry of nature," but he goes on to say that in such a poetry, "...there is a willingness to approach the living creatures with the kind of attentiveness that is almost a reverence. In Robert Bly's poems about nature he is at his best and most beautiful. Many of his ideas, political or religious or whatever, are absorbed into the attention that he is paying visually and spiritually to the things he writes about. The ideas are all there in the poems about nature." Every time he says the word "nature" it means less and less. It's clear that "attentiveness" is at the center of the approach, however, but that seems to be the case for any kind of poetry worth its words. Thus: all of these descriptions just come back to words. I wish I knew how to tell you. The worst poems are those with descriptors stuck to them, just like the worst poems are those that strive so hard to describe that they fail to capture.

If this poem is a nature poem, it's also a political poem, a love poem, an experimental poem, an elegy, a eulogy. What all of these hope to capture is an awareness — a product of attentiveness — that all of your efforts to exert control — over one another, over the mysteries of passion and romance, over the natural world, over language itself, over death — amount to little more than strength-training for the bloated ego that's sensitive to touch, on the verge of rupture, that part of you that makes you preconditioned to see yourself as a poet. The beauty in this poem, the meaning I find in it, is the poet coming to understand the joy that such a realization gives way to once you relinquish that control and the desire for it.

All is play. This poem about loss giving way to emptiness, then, is filled with happiness, that cliche of bad poetry and the missing piece in the cliches of so-called serious poetry.

What has always struck me about Jim's attempts at so-called "nature poems" is that the common theme between them is description. When they succeed, as some of them do in his later work, they capture the scene of squirrels scampering, or the chicken hawk circling above his hammock, rather than merely describing what he sees, which reduces it to words. This may very well be the ultimate test of all poems — describe or capture — but for the sake of my rumination on this poem memorializing me, it occurs to me that the goal for criticism appears to be the exact opposite: successful criticism should be, first, a description, that is, an accurate and exhaustive view of what is going on in the poem. If you can't describe what the poem is, what it looks like and sounds like and what occurs in it, you are bound to fail in trying to analyze or interpret it, which are forms of capture.

As his go-to critic for many of these nature poems and his poems in general, I told Jim bluntly during our training sessions when his drafts of poems suffered from one of the following: sometimes they were pages of ill-earned or immature capture that came across as superficial or sentimental because the capture hadn't been preceded by — worked out through — description; other times (most of the time) he would undertake the description with rigor, but his pride as a poet got in the way of moving it out of the way, as I would harp on him, to make room for the capture, which is all that matters in the end. On days when he'd had less to drink by the time he came to me, he'd hear me out and we would stomp and trudge toward better drafts of what he had. On days when he'd started drinking with or without Bly first thing in the morning, deluded into thinking the best poems would be found at the bottom of a bottle, he'd quit our training after we'd barely gotten started. Unable to describe through the slur, let alone capture anything in his shaky hands, he'd throw to the ground the pages he'd brought over, pick up his empty mason jar, and sulk off, muddy all over and flushed with sweat.

7

This poem, "In Memory of the Horse David, Who Ate One of My Poems," represents the pinnacle of Jim's career precisely because of its reluctance toward a one-size-fits-all climax. Without getting too far afield, it's worth noting the trajectory of his work leading up to the *Collected Poems*. In his first two books, *The Green Wall* and *Saint Judas*, the reader encounters a young poet who has, I would argue, mastered the craft: the poems are deftly laid out on the page with a keen ear for rhythm and meter. Of the selection from these two books that he shared with me, all of the poems scan: I remember beating my hoof in sync to their meter when he'd recite or read them during our training sessions. Most of them stick to a rhyme scheme, and many of them are sonnets, with the titular poem of the second collection being, perhaps, the most noteworthy. Skills aside, however, the poems didn't please him for long, as I've already touched on. He couldn't see a way to reconcile the freedom that poetry gives an individual with the constraints of formal, traditional verse. Even though he was an avid reader of Walt Whitman, his writing up until he arrived at Bly's farm was, like most of the mainstream poetry of 1950s America, staid, tied to conventional forms, and academic. The poets getting national recognition were not those descendants of Whitman pushing for free verse, let alone those seen as experimental, and the circle of poets Jim found himself in during and after his undergraduate studies at Kenyon College — Robert Penn Warren, John Crowe Ransom, Allen Tate, et al — were staunch New Critics, so it's no surprise that his first two books, published by Yale and Wesleyan, presses that are renown but academic not only in affiliation but in taste (and perhaps renown *because* they are academic), were not written in the Modernist strain of Pound and Williams. (Regarding academic presses: my hunch is that they all use the same printer, because in the poetry collections I've come across in my nearly twenty-five years, I have always been able to tell which books were published by academic presses because they have the same taste, a kind of artificial sweetness to the paper that must come from a dye their paper manufacturers use. It may or may not be due to this lingering flavor that many of the poems themselves might be described as saccharine, although it remains too difficult, at least for me, to separate taste from opinion.)

Considering his mastery of the sonnet, to say nothing of the so-called "square poem" he inherited from his more traditional clique at Kenyon, Jim's third book, *The Branch Will Not Break* (1963), is not the aberration that early critics tended to see it as, but a risk in bending his mastery of traditional verse just shy of its rupture. If you skim through the book, which is the reason, I would wager, why the name James Wright lives on, you quickly notice a pattern of surrealist flights of fancy, the so-called "Deep Image" lava lamp poems that consist of blobs of images, often green and/or dark in tone and obscure in shape or focus, that hover before the reader without a unifying effect other than the occasional parallelism of the images themselves. It's easy, especially to the reader with some hindsight, to see the influence of the European and Latin American poetics he'd thrown himself into, not only through his voracious reading, but also the translations he'd undertaken (some of them with Bly) of Spanish-language poets like Neruda and Vallejo, as well as the work of the Austrian poet Georg Trakl that he was drawn to precisely because he "didn't know what to do with it," yet saw that "it had a depth of life" that he needed, perhaps the depth missing from his second collection he characterized as leaving out, as I have already mentioned, so much of life. Much has been said about these influences and these image-oozing poems, but I want to talk about another pattern in the book: the poems' endings. (My jumping to their ends also comes down to the fact that I am still embarrassed by many of those poems, just as I was during the training sessions in which I would work on them with Jim, so I find myself short on praise for most of them. Here are some lines and phrases from those poems, language I couldn't help but laugh at: "suicidally beautiful" or "A bear under the snow / Turns over to yawn. / It's been a long, hard rest" (Okay, I neighed, what about it?) or "This cold winter / Moon spills the inhuman fire / Of jewels / Into my hands" (What does that even *mean*, Big Jim?) or someone strangling, if I remember right, "Under the black ripples of whitewashed walls" that made me want to strangle him with my bridle. As you'd expect, given these snippets of his poems, the majority of my training sessions with him came down to teaching him to refute sentimentality, a task so difficult that we had little time for me to train him in the finer points of poetic technique and tricks to increase the torque of his lines. He'd come to me with a fistful of lines or whole drafts of poems. He'd hand them over to me and I'd chew the words slowly, really breaking them down in my mouth. I'd spit most of them out and neigh, and that was enough for him to know he had work to do. On rare occasions, as with his "Lying in a Hammock" poem (although I spit out at least half of it, which, of course, he didn't cut), I'd swallow and then stomp, which was how he knew, he said, that he'd gotten the poem right. He'd neigh back in excitement, but his neighs weren't discernable to any horse's ears, so I'd stomp again to get him to stop and stick to his slurred words that I could, after all, understand. How difficult it was for him to realize that the enemy of clarity was not so much the surrealism he was under the spell of, but the sentimentality he couldn't, with all of his profound knowledge of poetic traditions, turn away from! If it sounds as though I'm writing from a pedestal above him, it's likely less from any feeling of my own superiority in poetic skill than a far more tangible feeling. Jim later claimed that the poems in *The Branch* are about his "rediscovery of the abounding delight of the body that I had forgotten about." If he came to remember that his body abounded in delight, where do you think he got that notion? He rode me until my already swayed back seemed sagging to my knees, swayed beyond belief. I abounded him toward that delight, and all I got in return was this poem saying I am dead. But back to what sets this poem — the poem in memory of me and the poem I ate — which continues to make me stomp, apart. Oh, I wish I'd had the chance to let him know, during his lifetime, that with this poem he'd finally taken to heart our training sessions!

Many of the poems in *The Branch* are a product of, rather than a break from, his formal expertise, particularly with their endings. This is perhaps a development of his extensive practice with the sonnet form, whose volta, that turn at the end, is seen to deliver what I would call the intended moment of ecstatic transfer of the poem. (Although being a formal move that recurs, it becomes prescription, meaning it becomes expected by the reader, meaning it's therefore less likely to transfer much of anything ecstatically to the reader.) Because of his close contact with traditional forms prior to the late fifties, his work from around the time he washed up at the Bly's farm retains traces of gestures like the volta. For instance, these three poems, probably the most enduring of the breakthrough collection:

LYING IN A HAMMOCK AT WILLIAM DUFFY'S FARM IN PINE ISLAND, MINNESOTA

Over my head, I see the bronze butterfly,
Asleep on the black trunk,
Blowing like a leaf in green shadow.
Down the ravine behind the empty house,
The cowbells follow one another
Into the distances of the afternoon.
To my right,
In a field of sunlight between two pines,
The droppings of last year's horses
Blaze up into golden stones.
I lean back, as the evening darkens and comes on.
A chicken hawk floats over, looking for home.
I have wasted my life.

BEGINNING

The moon drops one or two feathers into the field.
The dark wheat listens.
Best still.
Now.
There they are, the moon's young, trying
Their wings.
Between trees, a slender woman lifts up the lovely
shadow
Of her face, and now she steps into the air, now
she is gone
Wholly, into the air.
I stand alone by an elder tree, I do not dare
breathe
Or move.
I listen.
The wheat leans back toward its own darkness,
And I lean toward mine.

A BLESSING

Just off the highway to Rochester, Minnesota,
Twilight bounds softly forth on the grass.
And the eyes of those two Indian ponies
Darken with kindness.
They have come gladly out of the willows
To welcome my friend and me.
We step over the barbed wire into the pasture
Where they have been grazing all day, alone.
They ripple tensely, they can hardly contain their
happiness
That we have come.
They bow shyly as wet swans. They love each other.
There is no loneliness like theirs.
At home once more,
They begin munching the young tufts of spring in
the darkness.
I would like to hold the slenderer one in my arms,
For she has walked over to me
And nuzzled my left hand.
She is black and white,
Her mane falls wild on her forehead,
And the light breeze moves me to caress her long
ear
That is delicate as the skin over a girl's wrist.

Suddenly I realize
That if I stepped out of my body I would break
Into blossom.

Notice how all three poems hinge on the final line or two. Without them, there would be no *turn* in the poem, as with a sonnet's volta, and the reader would be left with little more than a smattering of images of nature, which wouldn't make a successful, or at least unified, nature poem. In Jim's words, "Human beings are unhappily part of nature, perhaps nature become conscious of itself. Oh, how I would love to be a chickadee! But I can't be a chickadee, all I can be is what I am. I love the natural world and I'm conscious of the pain in it. So I'm a nature poet who writes about human beings in nature. I love Nietzsche, who called man 'animal.'" (This gives you a sense of what I had to suffer through during our training sessions together.) These poems turn on the speaker's contact with the natural world, where his pain is reciprocated, as in the final lines of "Beginning": "The wheat leans back toward its own darkness, / And I lean toward mine." Or, that pain is relieved through contact with the natural world, as in the final lines of "A Blessing": after a giddy encounter with the two ponies, and the one in particular that seems to take to the speaker, it dawns on him "That if I stepped out of my body I would break / Into blossom." His body is what has him corralled, it appears, and the presence of loneliness that the speaker experiences between these two ponies who are fenced in and all alone mirrors, for the reader, the speaker's own sense of isolation. (A related matter of equine concern: in the poems of *The Branch*, he took our long faces too literally. I and others on the farm and on adjacent farms up and down the road, were reduced simply to a false correlation between a long face and negative emotions: sadness, loneliness, despair. We all had lugubrious faces. I tried to impress upon him that literal truth is the least valuable, the least generative, let alone interesting, form of truth. We live in a culture where, at all moments of the day, it seems, people think that the most profound point they can contribute to a conversation comes from reducing, or at least thinking they are reducing, their thoughts and experiences down to literal truths as opposed to poetic or figurative ones. (That is what the prevalence of the word "literally" in our culture shows us — literally.) But as you see smattered all over the poems in that book, he didn't quite get it. The horses are passive, despondent, are there for his comfort, and so forth and so on. That we are all and none of those things is what he couldn't quite get. And what's worse — if that book is said to be his best, what does this say about how the "reading" public perceives us?) The three poems reveal a speaker who has an acute understanding of suffering, not only as he experiences it in his own life, but as he sees it in the world in which he lives a life of suffering as all living things do. (No, I'm not a Buddhist. I'm a horse, and as such, moving through life without a tortured mind, I don't require further torture in the form of spirituality to reconcile suffering with peace. Let's stick to the poem.)

So, the volta of sonnets leads to his gesture toward closure in the poems of *The Branch Will Not Break*. They are daring, and indeed many of the poems' endings risk that Horatian unity — not to be confused with anything pertaining to horsely matters — he was tied to, which the rest of the poems' imagery often seeks to achieve, as in "Lying in a Hammock" and its rather abrupt shift with the final line. However, the poems as a whole still tilt toward rapture: they position the poet at the center, where he is expected to provide for the reader the Big Reveal, the moment in the poem that they might learn from before going on with their lives. This seems not only trite and presumptuous, but artificial and pastoral. At the time he was writing this and other poems for *The Branch*, for instance, there wasn't rapture so much as its opposite: the threat of nuclear war, on the one hand, and the fight over segregation and civil rights on the other. I hardly need to point out that a lyrical swan dive in a poem, that anachronistic wholeness and unity neatly wrapped up and delivered to the reader in the form of a poem, seems unlikely to be what American readers needed to get from poetry.

By the time he gets to this poem memorializing me, however, Jim has come to understand that rapture doesn't have a precise location in time and space on the page of a poem, just as it doesn't in life. Instead, continuing to build on the rupture he began toying with in *The Branch*, it seems he came to see that the only meaningful rapture, if any at all, is the one that occurs everyday, that converts us, at least briefly, from depressed into content in the dailiness of life, whether dramatic in its suffering or mundane in its tedium. What matters, and what you can see Jim has learned matters when you come to this poem in memory of me and the poem of his that I ate, is the rapture in those tiny moments that constitute our days: a clear evening's fully torched sunset that raises the brilliance of haystacks to a plain in flames; the taste of the first clover of spring that not only looks green but tastes it; the welcome of your stall once all the shit has been shoveled out and the piss has been covered over with fresh dirt and sawdust raked smooth. Since this poem about a lost poem and a dead horse doesn't end, it suggests that rapture is random and leads to nowhere but right back here. And this isn't a depressing conclusion, nor a throwing-up of hands in defeat, but a liberating awareness that in the well-worn paths of our quotidian ambling, in our passive lapping at the algae-streaked trough, lay the meaning of our galloping lives.

8

Then there are the words — on the other side of the page — you see through. They do not, as we might suspect at first, dilute the theme of emptiness but add to it. It is not the presence of those words in the following poem of the book that we see, when we read this poem, but their absence. I am struck with meaning when I come to a ghost line from the opposite side of the page passing into this one as through a wall. I note fugitive *b*s or *d*s or are they *p*s that I see amassing into the form of words when I hold the page up to the light. I can see the phantoms of lines in that poem hiding on the right margin of this one, huddling in quatrains, couplets, and tercets through the paper. I don't need to read the words and lines backwards, let alone translate them forwards, to know what they mean. The effect is that the emptiness in this poem — the loss of horse and poem —

comes not only from its lines, its language, but from where its lines and language are missing, impressed upon me all the more by the sight of that poem's trace in this poem's blank spaces.

You feel all the more acutely, when tracking a phantom word backwards as it slips onto this page, the passing of "the horse David" — who, again, is still very much alive, if further swaybacked and brittle in his old age — and the poet's despair over losing the poem. Naturally, this also suggests that every poem is connected, that what we mean by "poem" is not an isolated text but the whole book, in this case the *Collected Poems*, since meaning accrues from poem to poem as much as it does word to word, line to line. This is evidenced by the tradition of ordering a manuscript to get the most accrual or resonance across its pages, a practice that Jim, ever the brutal reviser and excisor of his poems, held close. He was fond of Robert Frost's quip (*not him again!* I'd stomp at the mention of such an icy name attached to such cold poems) that if you have a book of twenty-four poems, the book is the twenty-fifth. He brought this up at least three times, I remember, in our training sessions over the sequencing in *The Branch.* I can't speak to his process for ordering the *Collected Poems*, where this poem appears, since I didn't work with him on it: he was long gone from our side of the pasture by then, having moved in 1966, I gathered from Bly, to a spot of pasture of indeterminate quality that is among the first to greet the morning sun still soaking from the water it sleeps in. Some place he called Manhattan. A year later, Bly saw no use in keeping me around, since the farm was by then little more than a garden and yard that the young kids trampled all over. In hard times, Bly had sold off most of the farm to adjacent corn farmers, but warped as my back was by then, I had no stamina for hard work anyway. Almost always in pain, I had little patience for the goings-on around me and spent my days ambling around the barn, looking out at the pasture and the horizon of corn, and ambling some more once I gathered the strength to get moving. I bit one of the kids (I don't care to talk about it), and that was the last straw: he sold me off to a wheat farmer by the name of Jensen, who I've been with ever since, munching cast-off grains and chaff in the middle of the pasture's nowhere, somewhere Jensen calls Twin Crooks when he's grumpy and the feed is tight, but at least here I'm not bothered by insecure and drunken poets. As Jensen loaded me onto the trailer, I heard Bly, never one for business, say to the taciturn farmer that I probably didn't have much life left in me, so let's forget the haggling and you can give me whatever you want for an old horse you can't ride or work. I stared at Bly through the feed grate in the trailer and knew his poems would go no farther than his farm. He stared back as we took off, but he didn't even bother with a wave.

All that said, however, it's easy enough to gather some of Jim's process in putting the book together by sniffing around in it. The poem preceding this one in his *Collected Poems* ends with these lines, "...This poem is a little / Darkness for them, where they do not have to weep. / Not for me, anyway." It's plain to see how those lines from that poem, "Eclogue at Nash's Grove," reflect the lines of this poem memorializing me. Since this seems obvious, I'll say no more about it and try to stick to working through the poem in question — aside from stating that that poem, consisting of free-versed quatrains with the exception of two five-line stanzas, one of which is the final, and filled as it is with direct allusions to the emotions and experience it strives to transfer to the reader ("mourning," "standing on the dead," "grave," "elegy," "mourner," "mourn," "lives who are eaten away," "killed," and the aforenoted darkness and weeping are all included in the poem of forty-six lines) achieves far less in its slack, chatty lines than this poem does in its pulling taut the reader's attention toward emptiness through a minimalism that risks erasing the poem completely. That risk, I would remind Jim in our training sessions, is not only what holds the reader's attention tight, but it's also what tightens the poem. Once it's strained to the point of rupture, it's a clearer reflection of what the poet is meant to do. Why bother writing, I'd stomp at him when he'd give me such bad lines I'd carry their bitter taste around for days, if you aren't risking failure? I'd rather interpret the morning steam coming off my piss in the barn stall. He'd huff and puff and drink down the rotgut that he'd keep in that mason jar on the fencepost during our training sessions.

9

Lest this sequence in his book seem inconsequential, note that this is the same poet who said, following a notion I impressed upon him during one of our sessions, that "whatever else poetry is, it is a struggle, and the enemy, the deadly enemy of poetry is glibness." You can't know the meaning of glibness until you've had a spur in your side, a whip on your tail — these teach you, I was trying to show him, the power of concentrating actions, desires, and commands down to their essential message. Jim was also fond of claiming that his writing process typically began with a rhythm rather than an idea. "I don't know what I'm going to say, and three-fourths of the time after I've finished I don't even know what I've said." For the reader sniffing around in these two poems in the *Collected Poems*, it seems that his "Eclogue" was the first attempt at getting the rhythm of the idea down. He seems to notice, somewhere in the thick of the poem, that this is a rhythm in pursuit of emptiness, an elegiac rhythm, which critics would likely say is typical of his writing. With his head emptied of that feeling instilled by that rhythm, he starts to clean up the poem in order for the rhythm to match the idea. For me, at least, the final product of "Eclogue" remains glib, especially when read alongside the poem in my memory that follows it in the book: that poem, surely, gets the poet as close as he can get to vanquishing glibness. If I know what he's saying in the finished poem presented in the book, it's because he's gotten the thing down to the point where it's neither rhythm nor idea but a sustained effort, and a strained one, to keep glibness, that deadly enemy of poetry, at bay.

So, okay, I was in the chicken house, drunk on a poem and on the bourbon I'd swept out of Bly's liquor cabinet. Since I couldn't see the poem straight, through the inspiration of the bourbon, of the moment, of my ego, of the poem's ability — if it would amount to nothing more — to banish from my mind, pickled like my liver from drink, the marriage I was failing and the infant son of mine I was already forgetting, I had to take the poem to someone who could. This is why I didn't want to find someone to show the poem to.

I had to push myself away from the desk cursed with wonky legs that wouldn't stand firmly on the ground. I had to pull myself out of the chair. I teetered. I smoked Pall Malls because I was a sucker for sappy words and Pall Malls' tagline was "Wherever Particular People Congregate," the place in my ego where I counted myself king. My tarred fingertips and nails pointed to the state of my lungs that coughed up the smoke and coughed up the smell of chicken shit onto the poem on the desk in the typewriter I'd lugged from Minneapolis on the bus because I didn't drive.

Because I was short on money because I drank myself out of teaching jobs across colleges and universities in Minneapolis and because the little I was making from essays, reviews, and the sporadic teaching gigs I could find hours away from my reputation in the Twin Cities, was going to my wife, mortgage, child support, and Pall Malls and liquor, I folded my sheets of paper in half vertically, because then I would have four long sides, front and back, with margins wide enough for me to put my poems onto. Because my father worked his whole life in Martins Ferry, Ohio, in a factory forging mason jar lids, I preferred to drink out of mason jars. Because my father worked his whole life in that factory, and because my mother worked in an industrial laundry, I was a drunk, not an alcoholic. The jar I had in the chicken house was now empty, which was also why I teetered, and also why I teetered toward the door toward the farmhouse where I would show the poem to someone, where I would refill my jar.

10

In his introduction to the poem during that 1973 reading, Jim calls it a "poem — or something," something more than just a joke, and the fact that he cannot recognize it as a poem proper means nothing. Most writers have no idea what they are doing with words until the words huddle together and tell them what's going on. Jim, too, as he himself admitted, is not immune to bafflement in the face of one's attempts to domesticate language into something you can name and sway. Perhaps the one-fourth of the time remaining in his calculation noted above is the rare occasion when the "three-fourths" of that whole being that hovers over a poem — the writer — gets out of the way, or is forced out of the way, so that the humble "one-fourth" of what hovers over the poem — the reader — can sidle up to it and take a look. Perhaps writers would better understand what they were doing and what they have done if they allot at least two of those fourths to reading, allowing for each half, reading and writing, to have equal say in what is going on. Perhaps that is merely the start, though, and another marker of good poems is that they are created by writers who are composed of more than one-half of reading.

It's a matter, too, of coming to grips with where a poem resides. Does a poem live on the page, in the voice, in the air, stuck in your throat, or lodged in the grooves of your hooves until the farrier comes along and scrapes you clean? Jim and I spent countless sessions arguing over this. Ebullient reciter of poems that he was, what with his photographic memory and always having enough drink to keep him chatty, even if I could only understand what he was slurring a fraction of the time, he swore up and down that the poem doesn't exist until or unless it's given breath. And yet you write it on paper, Jim, I would stomp, to record where the breath is given! The poem, I was always trying to get through to him as he went on and on uninhibited by manners or booze, is what's in the space between words. That's what you're trying to scratch your way back into when you scrape your pen across the pages of your typewritten drafts. I remember him slurring at the trees, spittle at the corners of his lips, "I wonder where words are before anybody speaks them."

The problem with most poets is that they don't know that words are what you get out of the way of. You get out of their way. This is what my eating the poem was meant to teach him. This is what his writing of this poem, "In Memory of the Horse David, Who Ate One of My Poems," reveals he finally learned. This is why he smiled during that reading. This is why I am writing, as he was, in memory of what came before us, poems and poets, what we have to risk putting into words. I am trying to get to the bottom of all of the because.

NOTE

The biographical details relevant to the poem that this story deals with come from Jonathan Blunk's *James Wright: A Life in Poetry*, as well as comments Wright made during four interviews, all of which are gathered in his *Collected Prose*, and the audio archive of his 1973 reading at the University of Arizona.

ABOUT THE AUTHOR

Tyler Cain Lacy is also the author of a poetry chapbook, *Reus* (Press Board Press). He lives in the Bay Area.

Long Day Press

Recommended Titles

An Atavic Fear of Hailstorms
João Reis
Novella
ISBN: 9781950987290 • $14

Memory Field
Eric Tyler Benick
Travelogue
ISBN: 9781950987443 • $16

Saturn
Simon Jacobs
Stories
ISBN: 9781950987481 • $16

How to Adjust to the Dark
Rebecca Van Laer
Novella
ISBN: 9781950987207 • $16

www.ingramcontent.com/pod-product-compliance
Lightning Source LLC
Chambersburg PA
CBHW021727190726
48289CB00008B/2734

* 9 7 8 1 9 5 0 9 8 7 4 9 8 *